STINKY RIDDLES

by Katy Hall and Lisa Eisenberg

pictures by Renée Andriani

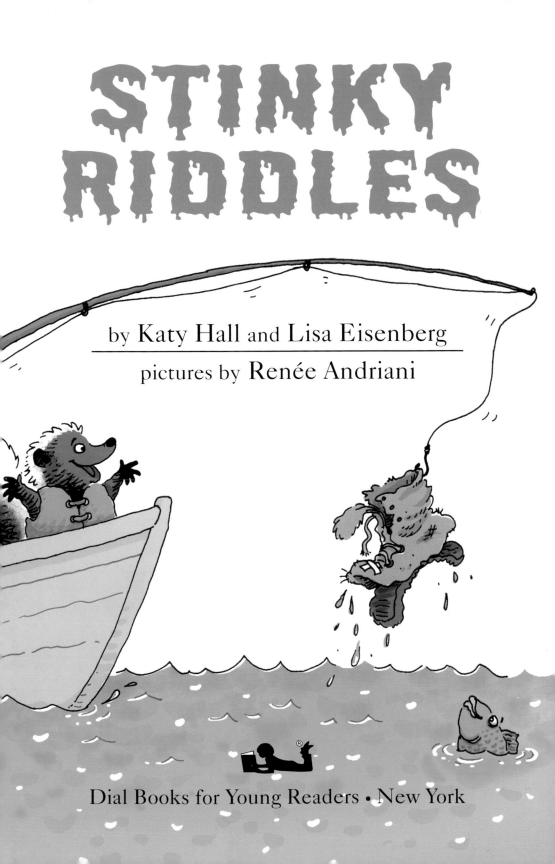

Dial Books for Young Readers • New York

DIAL BOOKS FOR YOUNG READERS
A division of Penguin Young Readers Group
Published by The Penguin Group
Penguin Group (USA) Inc., 375 Hudson Street, New York, NY 10014, U.S.A.
Penguin Group (Canada), 10 Alcorn Avenue, Toronto, Ontario, Canada M4V 3B2
(a division of Pearson Penguin Canada Inc.)
Penguin Books Ltd, 80 Strand, London WC2R 0RL, England
Penguin Ireland, 25 St. Stephen's Green, Dublin 2, Ireland (a division of Penguin Books Ltd.)
Penguin Group (Australia), 250 Camberwell Road, Camberwell, Victoria 3124, Australia
(a division of Pearson Australia Group Pty Ltd)
Penguin Books India Pvt Ltd, 11 Community Centre, Panchsheel Park,
New Delhi - 110 017, India
Penguin Group (NZ), Cnr Airborne and Rosedale Roads, Albany, Auckland 1310,
New Zealand (a division of Pearson New Zealand Ltd)
Penguin Books (South Africa) (Pty) Ltd, 24 Sturdee Avenue,
Rosebank, Johannesburg 2196, South Africa
Penguin Books Ltd, Registered Offices: 80 Strand, London WC2R 0RL, England
Text copyright © 2005 by Kate McMullan and Lisa Eisenberg
Pictures copyright © 2005 by Renée Andriani
Manufactured in China on acid-free paper
The Dial Easy-to-Read logo is a registered trademark of
Dial Books for Young Readers,
a division of Penguin Young Readers Group ® TM 1,162,718.

1 3 5 7 9 10 8 6 4 2

Library of Congress Cataloging-in-Publication Data
Hall, Katy.
Stinky riddles / by Katy Hall and Lisa Eisenberg ;
pictures by Renée Andriani.
p.   cm.
Summary: A collection of jokes, puns, and riddles about skunks.
ISBN 0-8037-2928-6
1. Riddles, Juvenile. 2. Skunks—Juvenile humor. [1. Skunks—Humor.
2. Riddles. 3. Jokes.] I. Eisenberg, Lisa. II. Andriani, Renée, ill. III. Title.
PN6371.5.H374 2005
818'.5402—dc22   2003014420

Reading Level 2.4

*The art was drawn with pen and ink, then scanned
and colored in Photoshop.*

For Lisa Eisenberg,
who wrote all the really stinky riddles
—K.H.

To Stinky, from Mom
—L.E.

For my sweet little stinkers:
Maggie, Ellen, and Joe
—R.A.

What rock and roll star do skunks
love?

Smell-vis Presley.

What did the judge say when
the skunks ran in?

"Odor in the court!"

How many skunks does it take
to make a really bad stink?

Only a phew.

How do you wash a skunk?

From as fur away as possible!

What do little skunks like to do after school?

Go to the spray-ground.

What do little skunks like to do after dinner?

Watch smelly-vision.

Why did the little skunks
follow their mother?

It was in-stinkt.

Why couldn't the little skunk
buy a gumball?

She only had one scent . . . and it was bad.

What would you get if you
crossed a skunk and a sheep?

A furry animal that smells really *baaaad*.

What do you call a skunk from another land?

A fur-eigner.

What did the skunk put on
before her date?

Per-*fume*.

Why didn't the little skunk
make the wrestling team?

He was too p.u.-ny.

What song did the Skunk Marching Band play?

"Stars and *Stripes* Forever."

Why did the skunk cross the
road?

Who nose?

What's black and white and red
all over?

A sunburned skunk.

Why did the little skunk act up in school?

He liked to be the scenter of attention.

Did the herd of skunks go that way?

No, they went the odor way.

What did the skunk say when
the wind changed?

"It's all coming back to me now!"

What do you call a skunk that comes in last at a skating competion?

The Stink of the Rink.

What did the umpire say when
the little skunk came up to bat?

"Three stripes and you're out!"

What position did the little skunk play on the baseball team?

Scenter field.

What story do little skunks like to hear at bedtime?

Winnie-the-Pew.

Where do skunks go for great spaghetti?

Aroma, Italy.

What part of kindergarten do little skunks like best?

Show-and-smell.

Are little skunks afraid of soap
and water?

I stink so!

What do you get if you cross a
bus with a skunk?

All the seats to yourself.

What is a little skunk's favorite
song?

"Stinkle, Stinkle, Little Star."

What do you call a skunk after you wash it in hot water?

A shrunk!

Why didn't the skunk and the pig get married?

They had too much common scents.

If a skunk has a stuffy nose,
how does she smell?

Terrible!

What do you get if you cross a
giant with a skunk?

A BIG stink.

What's black and white, has
four wheels and flies?

A skunk driving a garbage truck.

What plays loud music and
smells bad?

A skunk rock band.

What do you get if you cross a baby with a skunk?

I don't know, but I wouldn't want to change its diapers!